Tyrone
I DIN DO NUFFIN

Created and Written by
Charles Davis

In Loving Memory

of Graceson

Brylie Davis

Urban

HIP HOP

Free Writing

Express Yourself Creatively

Pineburg Times

Published 11/17/1990

The Deuces 22nd Street
Business District

Black business were thriving during the Jim Crow era of Pineburg, Fl. African American businesses boomed on 22nd Street. Art, music, food, and culture brought the locals together. Everything was in distance.

It was the only place blacks could go to without being discriminated. There were over 100 black business owners. Blacks spent money within the community. The Manhattan Casino was a popular sight for black musicians to perform. There was the Royal Theater down the road to catch a movie. Black lawyers and doctors operated along 22nd Street as well.

Pepper Town, Methodist Town, and Gas Plant District were once successful African American communities. Once the Civil Rights Act was passed, blacks began to leave the area. Black businesses that needed black dollars started to close down. Today, 22nd Street is known as Midtown that was once a popular attraction. Few businesses still stand.

275

South
Exit 30

Pineburg
Next Right

Table of Contents

WELCOME TO PINEBURG

Pigs

Racism

Criminals

Equality

City Manuel Hand Book

Tourist Guide

Track 1

Hot Wheels

It's HOT and the A/C unit is frozen. So, it's barely pushing any cool air out. The temperature in the house 80 and the A/C on 70. It feels like summer all year long in Pineburg, FL. Thirteen year old Tyrone Jenkins lay motionless on the couch stretched out. The alarm on his phone starts going off next to him. He's sleeping like a baby.

Floesha, Tyrone's mom, doesn't know how he can't hear his phone going off when it's beside 'em. She woke up mad and tired of having to wake him up. He's old enough by now to wake himself up.

"Turn that shit off! You waking up my house Tyrone. And getcho ugly ass up and get ready for school."

Tyrone doesn't hear her. He was having a wet dream about fucking a classmate. So she comes in the living room yelling, "GETCHO MOTHAFUCKIN ASS UP! GET UP!"

She goes into the kitchen without saying shit and fills a glass of cold water and dumps it over his head.

"I'm d-r-o-w-n-i-n-g," said Tyrone.

Tyrone nuts on himself.

"Now take yo' long headed ass to school," said Floesha.

"I'm not going today. I went yesterday."

"I wish I was yo' got damn step mom."

Floesha noticed Dae Dae her youngest son's drawers were wet.

"I know damn well yo' stupid, dirty, pissy, dehydrated ass spose to be on yo' air mattress sleeping on my flo." She picks his drawers up with a metal hanger.

"WHAT THE FUCK! Bitch! Get this nasty shit out my house." And she slap 'em, with the wet drawers.

"Getcho ass up and mop that shit off my flo. And don't use to much of that mothafuckin bleach."

Dae Dae gets up.

"I didn't pee," he stuttered.

He won't tell you he pissed.

"Act fucking retarded if you want to," said Floesha.

Dae Dae sleeps on the floor next to Tyrone. He has a bladder problem. The doctors told Floesha the only thing she could do is wait for him to grow out of it. There's pretty much nothing they can do and he's 8. Floesha don't want him sleeping on her furniture.

Tyrone is mad as hell, getting ready for school. He goes in the bathroom and just pisses any kind of way like there aren't any women in the house. Piss gets on the toilet.

Tyrone doesn't even clean it up or wash his hands. He goes into his sister's room to get his clothes. They both share the same dresser. His little sister gets the top drawer while Tyrone gets the bottom. After Tyrone gets his clothes, he goes into the hallway closet to get his shoes.

He grabs them and put 'em, on. Tyrone asks his mama can he eat a pop tart before he leave. She told 'em, he need to go to school on time and eat they free food.

"Can't even feed your own child. SMH I'm bout to go. I need the house key."

Floesha don't wanna give 'em, one. She don't trust him as far as she know. Tyrone irresponsible.

"I paid for the mothafucka," said Floesha, an find a reason why she don't wanna give 'em, one.

"Next time you try to come in my house at 3:30 in the morning like you grown don't come here. Stay yo' ass where you at."

Tyrone dressed in his school uniform leaves his house headed to the bus stop. He lives on the top half of a 2 story duplex. Tyrone walks down the steps and goes to the front.

"What up?"

He sees Baldie, the neighbor who share the same property with him, nods his head.

Baldie don't never speak to Tyrone. Every time he try to speak to him he always nods his head.

Baldie starts thinking his thoughts out loud while smoking a joint on the side of his house. "These kids starting to become pests around my yard throwing trash." He picks up the trash.

Tyrone thinks his mom has issues, and she thinks Tyrone is the issue. They argue about everything.

He never knows when to shut the fuck up. Tyrone is walking down the sidewalk and decides not to catch the bus. Instead, he goes back home to get a bike he stole from white people off their porch. Skinny tire riders - that's what the hood call 'em.

He jumps on the bike and rides to the gas station. Blind man Twan, who stays next to Baldie, comes outside telling Amena and Cordell to getcho ass in the house now!

After no response, Twan goes to the back yard and angrily shouts, "HEY, BRING Y'ALL ASS INSIDE NOW!" Cordell and Amena stand in front of Uncle Twan giggling and not saying anything.

Twan has a hearing problem too.

Tyrone rides his bike down the sidewalk towards the gas station. All while scouting for a victim. "Bingo! I guess his old ass is going to need a walker now."

An old white man was pumping gas. When the man was done, Tyrone had his plan in effect. He flags down the old man and tells him his tire is flat.

"Hello! Excuse me, sir," said Tyrone.

"Hello," said the old man.

"Sir, you have a flat tire right there," pointing towards the rear passenger tire.

"Right where? Let me see, let me get out right quick I don't see it."

When the man gets out to check, Tyrone circles the car and drops his bike to jump in the driver's seat.

"My mama said she would see you in church this Sunday."

"You mean she would be seeing you in a casket," said the old man. Tyrone speeds off at 30 miles an hour, inches away from running the man over. He drives to his neighborhood and rides by the bus stop just to stunt. Flaunting money and smoking weed.

Sticking his head out the window, he jerks the wheel from side to side. Tyrone takes a selfie smoking a joint while holding the car keys he stole. He calls them his trophies. Tyrone posts his picture on social media, doing it for the likes.

The old man calls the police. "911 operator, what's your emergency, city, and state."

"Pineburg, FL. I would like to report my car has been stolen."

The operator transfers him over to Pineburg Police Department. "Pineburg Police Department what's your emergency and location?"

"I'm over here at the gas station, Snacs to Crac, and my car has been stolen."

"Ok. We're sending officers to your location."

"Thank you."

The old white man goes into the store and waits for the police.

"Sir, my car has been stolen from your gas station. Do your cameras work."

"Oh wow! I'm sorry this happened to you. Did you call the police?"

"Yes, I just did," said the old man.

"Have you ever been a victim of a reverse robbery?"

"No. What do you mean?"

"Give me all your money if you want the tapes." Dispatch bursts over the radio in the officer's patrol car.

"We have a report of an old dumb ass who left his keys in the car and now he can't find it. Warning signs - may include dementia. Subject's prior location, Snacs to Crac. Proceed with caution, over."

The old white man waves down the police when he sees them. Two police cruisers park by the vacuum cleaner then get out and stand in front of their car.

"Are you the old sock that lost your car?" said the male officer.

With his hand on his fire arm. "Easy big fella," while the old man approaches the officers.

"Well, this kid comes up to me he looks to be about 12 and tells me I have a flat tire. I didn't think nothing of it. He was so young. He was just a kid, you know. But sure old boy he fooled me. I got out and checked my tire, but I didn't see a problem. He told me it was the tire on the passenger side. I went around to see and the next thing i knew, he jumped off his bicycle into my car. I tried to chase him, but I'm too old."

"My dear, you appear to be suffering from hallucinations and dementia. Where is your care taker."

"I'm not crazy. My car was stolen."

"Are there any surveillance cameras?" said the officer.

"Well, I don't know. Is there?"

The store clerk raised an eye brow at the old man.

With loud music playing and smoke flowing out the windows, Tyrone pulls into a teacher's parking space with a stolen car. He is already late to school so no one sees him. Tyrone walks down the hallway to class, he spots one of his homeboys in a classroom.

He starts clowning around talking to the students by the door. Shining a laser on the teacher's ass when she's writing on the board. She turns around and he puts it on her forehead. The class laugh he gets busted by a hall monitor.

"Tyrone come here and stop disrupting classrooms."

Tyrone sees Ms. Speas and starts running, not thinking she would follow him, but she did. Right into the boys' bathroom. She calls for him to answer.

"TYRONE come out here. I know you're in there. Come out of there!"

Tyrone doesn't say a word.

"Tyrone! Answer me! I know it's you. I saw you come in here."

Just as Tyrone was laughing to himself in the stall, she pushes open the stall door. He's busted. Tyrone screeched, sounding like a little girl.

"What are you doing I'm peeing! I Din Do Nuffin."

"You're lying. Don't give me that crap. I saw you run into the bathroom. Don't call me a liar."

"I never said you was lying. You saying that, Ms. Speas."

"Come on with me to Dr. Cedric's office. You're late."

So now, before Tyrone even started school, he was on his way to the principal's office. When he got there, all Dr. Cedric could do is shake his head.

"He was just being his useless, brainless, idiotic self," said Ms Speas.

"Alright thanks a lot I'll take it from here. Tyrone in my office again, late again. What's your lie this time so I can write you a white note for always being late. I don't know how you get things done with no school supplies. You can't be doing your work. I can't let you slide this time, homie. You got to want to do better."

Dr. Cedric writes Tyrone a tardy slip and walks Tyrone to class to make sure he made it there. Tyrone walks into his first period math class.

"Tyrone you're late again. What's your excuse this time? Smoking gods lettuce," said his math teacher, Mr. Cardwell.

"You need to know math to sell grams."

All Tyrone can do is look at Mr. Cardwell with a stone-cold stare. He is high as a MOTHAFUCKA, acting like he doesn't hear the teacher talking to him.

He's grinning going to his desk, smelling like weed.

"Sorry i'm late. I left all my shit in your bedroom, Mr. Cardwell."

Mr. Cardwell's eyes zoom in on Tyrone's lips and all he could hear in slow motion was, "Your wife said you had a baby dick, Mr. Cardwell." Tyrone laughs in his face.

The class starts laughing, bringing memories back to Mr. Cardwell. Mr. Cardwell's face turns red, "Never talk about my wife, you son of a bitch. I feel bad for your mama. I didn't know a little shit could come from the front side."

"What you said about my mama?" Mr. Cardwell slowly calms down by squeezing the hell out of an anger management toy.

Squashing it picturing it's Tyrone brains everywhere, before he loses it and focuses himself. Mr. Cardwell lectures the class on an assignment. It didn't even last long before Tyrone starts distracting someone else. Tyrone instigated Buck and Javon to flame each other.

Tyrone likes to laugh from them ripping each other every day. They had to make it fun. Mr. Cardwell's class was boring.

"Hey look,"Tyrone points something out to Markeis Mc Glockton, a funny kid.

Tyrone switches his paper and erases Markeis's name. He gave him a blank piece of paper while his head was turned. The principal gets on the intercom, "Good morning, children. I want to say it is lovely to be a principal to all you angels. You all are so perfect that this morning we are getting a special guest appearance from the Pineburg Police Department. Because one of you scums, I mean angels, decided to steal a car and discard it on school grounds."

Tyrone is becoming a serious disruption, talking over the intercom.

"Tyrone, if you don't stop disrupting class, I'm going to have a private conference with your mother, and ho ho, you don't wanna know what I say in private conferences," said Mr. Cardwell, while looking over his glasses.

"I Din Do Nuffin. That's what you want me doing," said Tyrone.

"I'm going to call your mother, Tyrone."

Tyrone laughs at him.

"Go right ahead. But before you try, you gotta go down to the phone company and pay the bill first."

The whole class lost it, rolling. Mr. Cardwell is pissed Tyrone was always getting to him.

"Today is report card day, and you know what that means for you, Tyrone? DOOMS DAY! I mean report card day. Come get your future, I mean reviews."

"Fuck You!"

"I beg your mother."

"How did I get all F's, Mr. Cardwell? I do my work."

He walks back to his desk, puts his head down and takes a nap. Dreaming about being a rapper on stage in front of a huge crowd. Mr. Cardwell day dreams about taking his work shirt off and knocking Tyrone ass out like a man. He's past the point of it being a job and began to wonder if Tyrone wants to really fight him. Tyrone got so much mouth to be a little boy. The school not paying him enough for the level of disrespect.

Tyrone heads to 2nd period gym class with Mr. Frankel. Tyrone never dresses out for gym, but today was an exception.

"We have pictures today in the library," said Mr. Frankel.

"So everyone stand in a single file and shut up. When we get there, sign in and wait to be called. Quiet!"

As students start to form a line, Tyrone meets Lil Nick at the back of the line to sell him a sack. "I got stupid gas on deck."

"You straight with 4 dollars? This all I got." Tyrone knows he buying a gar with the other dollar.

"You good. Get my number. I'm T man." That's his drug dealer name he gives every body, and they did a transaction.

"Nick, where you from."

"I stay in the bricks, but I'm moving."

Nick claimed the bricks only because his friends started claiming it. He lived in the apartments for a year. Tyrone knows jits from the bricks be hitting all the time. And Nick was on that. He was about that life on some gangster shit. That's what peeked Tyrone's interest.

Nick told stories about dogging the police in stolen cars and how good he can drive at 14. Tyrone started treating the situation like some type of competition. And you know what that means? Two minds alike, think alike. The two of them talked the whole way to the library.

Mr. Frankel leads the kids into the library to sign in. An of course, Tyrone can't follow directions ever and signs in as Harry Azcrac. He went to a table and waited to be called. The librarian had to tell Tyrone to use his inside voice more than once. So she told Mr. Frankel to make him stop talking all together. He makes Mr. Frankel so mad, he starts to stomp his feet.

"Last but not least," and before the photographer could catch himself, he said, "Harry Azcrac." Everyone starts dying laughing. Tyrone goes up and takes a picture with his eyes closed making a retarded face. Mr. Frankel makes Tyrone walk with him on the way back to gym.

"I have my eye on you."

"Careful, Mr. Frankel. You stare at me too long, you might become a sex offender."

Last period bell rings, and Tyrone rides the bus home. The bus is loud and packed with kids talking over each other. Some kids are not assigned to the bus but sneak on it anyway. But it doesn't matter.

The bus driver, Jesus, a Spanish guy who the kids call baby Jesus because of his long beard and hair, never talks. He just drives. Tyrone sits on the back of the bus. He rolled a joint in the bathroom before the last period bell rang. So he fires it up and blows the smoke out of the window so the driver can't smell it. Tyrone listens to music on his phone, singing out loud. Then, he stands in the corner of his seat, whips his dick out and starts pissing on the bus. No home training what so ever. Baby Jesus keeps on driving like he doesn't see shit.

Tyrone gets home from school and his mom asks him where his homework is. Tyrone makes up a lie quick. "Oh, I already did it at school. They barely give any homework."

"But you never have any homework, Tyrone. And I never see your report card show me your report card."

"We din get our report cards today."

"I know you're failing because they sent me 3 copies of your report card. This week last week and the week before in the mail. I just wanted to see if you was gone lie. Y'all got report cards today, witcho lien ass. You got all F's. I should kick yo' ass at the bus stop in front of everybody so all your friends would see and cut you bald head."

"But ma, I Din Do Nuffin."

"I don't know what's up with this new generation. Back in the days, we stayed getting homework."

Tyrone starts playing the game, and he can't even be in the house for 20 minutes, when his mama is already screaming for him to clean up. Tyrone was focusing on the game so much, he ignores the queen of the castle even though she know he can hear her. Floesha comes in the living room and unplugs the video game and TV.

She's old school and that gets his attention. Tyrone told his mama she was aggravating. "What the fuck you said? Who the fuck you think you talking to?" Floesha cold cocked Tyrone's ass. "Witcho slick ass mouth, always got something to say back."

Tyrone only responds to violence. You can't be nice to kids these days.

"Ma! I Din Do Nuffin! I wasn't talking to you!"

"Then who you talking to?"

Tyrone gets up mad cleaning the house halfway through. He hauls ass because he feels one chore is like 1000 chores.

Tyrone heads to the block with weed in his back pack. People always piling up under a tree at his friend granddad's house.

Mr. Jake the snake is what they call him because he likes to call the police on them for always hanging out and selling drugs around his house. Them niggas don't do it around their mama's house. Mr. Jake called the police so many times, they had a blind warrant placed in front of his house. If the police saw people standing there in a group, they would be able to rush you. Mr. Jake was always coming out his front door telling Cortez's friends, "You know the police watching y'all now. They don't want you standing in front of my house. Cortez get your friends now."

"Y'all come down to the alley," said Cortez. "Blind warrant my ass thinking we don't know Jake the snake troll as fuck," said Tyrone.

So they would move down the alley for a minute and come back to stand in front of his house. Tyrone's phone rings. "Hello! Yeah, I'm good. How much? Meet me at the spot."

There was an alley next to Mr. Jake's house that Tyrone sent his traffic to. He named it after himself, Tyrone Boulevard. The only way to be safe at Cortez granddad's house was paying his grandma, Ms. Jesse, $20 or buying her a pack of beer every now and then.

Since Tyrone is always getting into trouble, he got his AK-47 hidden under Mr. Jake's house to protect the block. He wants to keep at least a gun on the block. Thugga and Bre are double trouble. They are a couple of Tyrone's homeboys. They never go to school. They are known for hitting licks together. If they had a house, they could fill the whole mothafucka up with stolen shit.

Thugga used to be an outstanding football player, but the street life got to him early. Bre is from Sun Peak Projects. He grew up in Tyrone's neighborhood as well. So, it's his second home. Lil

Nick rode his bike from across town on his way to his auntie's house. Nick sees Tyrone in the mid part of town, so he rides his bike over to him. Nick start hanging with Tyrone. Tyrone brought Nick to the hood. They spent the evening on the block smoking and drinking. Talking and clowning. Tyrone wanted to carjack someone when it got dark. Him and his friends go to the gas station an post up on the wall watching traffic go by. They chill on the wall for a minute.

Tyrone and his homeboys are watching the cars coming to and from the store. They need to find someone slipping, but they don't. After an hour, nothing seems to be happening. Tyrone grows impatient.

He was going to run out from behind the store's dumpster on somebody. It's a blind spot that didn't seem to work out either. They left the gas station and went to the next neighborhood over. They spot a nice car with a older man in it. The car was sitting in front of a house. Tyrone and his friends sneak up and pull guns on the driver.

"Fuck nigga don't move. You already know what it is."

"Man, I ain't got nothing. I got kids. Come on. You don't want to do this."

"Shut yo' dumb ass up! I do want to do this."

Tyrone pistol-whip the man and hit him one time. Blood starts leaking from his face.

"You broke my nose! Man, let me go to the hospital. I won't tell nobody, just let me go to the hospital."

Thug went into the mans pockets, while Bre jumps in the passenger seat. They threw the guy out into the road. Tyrone and his friends carjack and rob the driver. What they didn't know was the guy they just robbed happens to be a former drug lord. Tyrone forgets to turn on the headlights and drives off in the car. The man uses a phone close by to call the police.

"Hello 911 operator. What's your city, state, and emergency," said the female dispatcher.

"Hello, I need Rambo over here. These mothafuckas just hit me in the nose so hard, i'm bleeding worse than a night of doing too much coke."

"Sorry, sir. Do you need an ambulance or a drug counselor?"

"The bathroom," while he's wiping blood from around his mouth with his shirt.

"What's your location, sir? We can send EMS."

"3 feet from death."

"Welcome to marriage," said the dispatcher.

"Pineburg, FL," said the victim.

"Ok, I'm sorry sir. You're outside of our delivery zone." The phone goes silent.

The neighborhood is known for car thefts and burglaries. Tyrone and his friends are going back to the hood. When they get back, they all search the car for items they can sell front to back. They turn the A/C on full blast thinking it will kill the finger prints, since Nick doesn't wear any gloves. That's because he's never been in the system before. After they search the vehicle, Tyrone went to get his AK-47 and started shooting it in the air.

Doing stupid shit for attention. The gun is bigger than him. One of the older lame niggas who be hating and selling drugs around this bitch. Heard gun shots and came outside to see what's going on.

He seen a bunch of jits crowded around a vehicle. And calls the police. They making the neighborhood hot. Tyrone speeds out of control through the neighborhood. Joy riding, running stop signs and even slamming into one. They flew past an undercover cop sitting in a parking lot of a empty building. He notices a car speeding without any headlights on. Tyrone stops at a red light in the right lane.

As the cop slowly approaches the red light in the left lane. He can't see anyone driving. So he let down his window to get a good visual. When he looks down, he sees a little boy with a baby face driving the car. Can't be over 13 years old. Tyrone notices a plain clothes officer with his badge around his neck. He panic and speeds off.

The officer gets on his radio transmission and tells nearby officers he's in pursuit of a fleeing vehicle driving with their head lights off. That may be a child.

"The driver looks like Gary Coleman with a booster seat, over."

"We are going to get him quicker than the west coast got biggie, 10 4."

"Is 2pac there? Do you request assistance?" The undercover cop radios dispatch about chasing the suspects.

The police department made it clear this year they would stop chasing fleeing vehicles due to crashes.

"Don't fucking move until a donut shop opens."

Dispatch want the officer to stay put but the Pineburg Police do what they want and chase you anyway. The officer turns his dash cam and siren off and chases the car. Tyrone eludes the officer and runs into another one.

"Oh shit, troll. I'm bout to dick 'em."

He hit a left and a right and bucked that light. He is playing a cat and mouse game with these officers. The police officer lost sight of the stolen vehicle.

"I need to stop drinking on the job."

"Tim, you're a fucking loser, over."

"We need to block off all routes and possible exits." More officers began to circle the perimeter. Tyrone and his homeboys speed through the back roads and jump back on the main road.

"We have a stolen vehicle driving north bound over." The officers spot the car and start chasing them onto the interstate. The police couldn't catch them.

"We need the eagle in the sky." The police call in the Pineburg Eagle, a police helicopter. The chase makes the news. Tyrone is driving erratically, trying to stay ahead of police. K9 unit and patrol officers are setting spike traps.

"Eagle 1, we have a visual on the suspects driving at a high rate of speed. Speeding among traffic. It looks like they are in a sports model vehicle." Tyrone takes the nearest exit.

"I'm going to follow them so they can't get away."

"Give the police a little advantage," said the pilot. "Does this thing come with missiles, roger that."

"Now, they appear to be getting off exit 21. The suspects are looking to make a right turn. There's heavy traffic in both lanes. They go for it and is boxed in by cars. They are trying to drive around motorist but they can't move. The teens cut across the lanes onto the opposite side of the road."

"This could end very dangerous forthem and oncoming traffic," said the pilot.

Tyrone has the pedal to the metal, causing drivers to slam onto there brakes to avoid a head on collision.

"It looks like the suspects are picking up speed," said the pilot. He is at least doing 50 in a 35 and turns into a neighborhood.

"They almost hit a parked car on the road," said the pilot.

Tyrone smashing in PA Bricks neighborhood, also known as Pineburg Apartments. They cut through Sun Peak Projects and take the police crosstown. Tyrone gets by a middle school where they should've hopped out the car and tried to get away. But didn't, instead they drove inside a gulf course down the road.

"The suspects have now come to a complete stop," said the pilot.

They are cornered by the cops, so they ditch the car and jump the fence that separates the golf course and the canal. The helicopter pilot had to use infrared to see the suspects running along the mangroves. Tyrone sees an undercover cop circling the perimeter. He tries to out run the officer but is so dehydrated and tired from running in the canal that he got caught running in slow motion.

His clothes were wet and heavy. The officer hit Tyrone in the back of the head 3 times with his pistol and hand cuffs him. Tyrone tells the police "I Din Do Muffin," slurring his words. "I was conching. Y'all got the wrong nigga. I'm only 13."

"Then where's your bucket," said the officer.

"I Din Do Nuffin! Let me go." He tried to resist.

"We have 1 suspect in custody, over." Tyrone was the first to get caught. Lil Nick runs out of the canal into a wooded area and into a backyard. He hides his drugs inside a flower pot so he could come back and get it. Then he jumps into a recycling bin that was half way full of trash. The officers use the trash can to jump the fence of the backyard he was in because the gate was locked. When they searched the yard, the police found Lil Nick hiding in the bin.

"Freeze! Put your hands up and get down on the ground!"

Lil Nick starts smiling. They cuff and search him for any weapons.

"I could've sworn he had something in his hand."

"Did you see anything?"

"No, I haven't seen him toss anything."

"Ok check the area to make sure he hasn't thrown anything."

"We have a second suspect apprehended."

The police left a dent in the garbage can and never moved it back to where it was. Thugga, the 3rd suspect, ran out of the canal into the neighborhood. The K9 unit and the Pineburg Eagle chase him. A brief pursuit breaks out on the back road. The police try to tase him in the neck, but it flew past him when he looks back at the officers. He ran around a house that sits on the corner where a group of people were standing. Instead of running straight to get away, Thug runs around the house next to it and gets caught on the side of the house like a fool.

Thugga was arrested and put in a police cruiser. Bre was the 4th suspect to be arrested. There were so many police in the area he had nowhere to run. He was afraid to go in the canal because of the alligators. He thought he might have to wait hours before he could leave the way the police were looking for them. The eagle in the sky had seen Bre trying to hide in the mangroves and sent the police to his location. Bre was apprehended a short time after trying to stay in one spot. All four of them were detained and charged with numerous offenses. They were all taken to Pineburg Juvenile Detention Center, without further incident.

"Bill Boner reporting live on PWN News Pineburg World Networks, where four juveniles who are in custody lead police on a dangerous high-speed chase. The suspects carjacked, robbed, and beat the black off the victim. The chase ended inside The Urban League Golf Course, where the suspects abandoned the vehicle and fled on foot. All four were apprehended a short time later. Great job, Pineburg Police Department. Thank you for your hard work."

"Chief of Police, Keith Scott is live on the scene."

"There's been a series of crimes in the neighborhood. We urge Pineburg residents who live in the area to protect their vehicles by locking their car door. It's illegal to leave your car running at the gas station. Most people don't know that, so turn your vehicle off all times when exiting your vehicle. Unfortunately, kids steal cars and lead police on high speed chases. There's been an increase in juvenile carjackings and deaths. We need this trend to stop. Pineburg needs this to stop."

"Chief, what are the suspects being charged with or have you brought any charges at this point," said a reporter.

"I believe all four suspects are being charged with armed carjacking, armed robbery, reckless driving, driving without a valid license, aggravated battery, and possession of a firearm. That's just to name a few. More charges will be brought forth as well. These kids think it's a game until some one gets killed. The law protects these punks i mean individuals that pose a threat to the community. Repeat offenders should be direct filed and quit given slaps on their wrist. We wouldn't have this problem. They would think differently about what they're doing. I guarantee you. The laws are much leaner on juvenile offenders. They think they're invincible. Pineburg Police Department no more questions or comments until further investigation. Thank you."

"Ruby Cummings, We have a cold case of bread smelling like your dead grandma house with clothes stacked to the ceiling."

Track 2

First Day Out

Tyrone ended up doing 21 days. His mama wanted him to cop out to the charges. She said she was tired of going to court. Didn't give a damn if he was guilty or not. His mama gave him that tough love. Lil Nick was fighting for community service, since it was his first time going to JDC. The state wanted to send Thugga and Bre to a program for 9 months. Everybody was waiting on Tyrone to jump.

All of Tyrone's friends had already been released and waiting on court dates. Floesha's car broke down and she didn't have any money to pick up Tyrone from jail. So, she calls the sheriff's office and told them there was no way she can get her son. "I don't have a ride."

The deputy tells her the next time this happens we won't have a ride or any gas money to bring him home either. "Your son came to jail on his own ma' am."

Tyrone was released and dropped off in a white van. He got home 2 shades lighter and took a shower to wash the jail water smell off his body. The jail house processed reclaimed water that'll have your skin itching and breaking out in bumps.

Tyrone took an hour long shower and he's only so big wasting water. Floesha made him get his ass out the tub. She's tired of talking to Tyrone about going to jail because he gone do what he want regardless of what you tell him.

Tyrone calls Thug about a pair of gym shorts he let him hold. He doesn't really have any clothes, probably less than a week's worth, and he keeps wearing the same shit over and over. He don't have it like that. Tyrone was hungry, so he asks his mom for something to eat. She told him he better cook his ass some oodles and noodles in the cabinet.

"I don't feel like it!" There was a month's supply of noodles. Tyrone goes to the sink.

His mama mixed water in the dish soap. So the dishes not really being clean properly. Tyrone washes a bowl out, boils himself some beef noodles and mixes it with hot sauce. He eventually leaves without saying shit to a grown up.

Tyrone heads to the block. The block dry as hell, nobody's out. Tyrone talks to himself while walking to the corner store, Novels. A couple of people are standing outside the store. "C," said Tyrone.

"Slow motion ain't nothing," said Corey. Corey was an old head who was at the store a lot. Tyrone goes into the store and asks Tyree, the store owner, to sell him a gar. Tyree knows Tyrone is under age and told him to get the fuck out the store. Then calls him a shenjing bing.

"The police are on their way. Don't stand outside the door. Move."

"Shut the fuck up, Tyree. Always talking all that shit."

Tyrone doesn't see anyone inside so he goes outside and asks C to buy him a gar. Ty knows Tyrone's little tricks of asking people outside the store to buy him gars. Ty tells people not to buy gars for him. They don't wanna go to jail behind him.

Tyrone goes to Thug's house. Thug stays in the same neighborhood as him. Tyrone pulls up to his house and knocks on the door. Thug's mom answers.

"Hey, ma. Charles home?"

"He in there, Tyrone. You can come in."

"How you and your mom doing."

"She good. She at the house."

Tyrone goes to Thug's room all the way in the back. They sit down and play the game for a little while then get missing. Tyrone and Thug go to Bre's house, but he isn't there. So, they go back to Tyrone's and sit inside Floesha's broken down car. Tyrone rolls up a big doobie and they fog that mothafucka up. ZOOTED! Eyes are red as hell. They talk about stupid shit like broke hoes, bummy niggas, and who gets the most money. All kinds of irrelevant shit. Tyrone gets out to go feed his dog one scoop of dog food, which always gets eaten by the squirrels and birds.

Tyrone gets back in the car and asks Thug do you know anywhere we can get pit bull puppies. He wants to sell them to make money. Thug tells him they can sell 'em, but he wants to keep one. Thug wants to fight one against his cousin's dog. He thinks his dog is a killer. Scooby Doo is a deformed mutt. The mama had sex with her brother out the same liter. So Scooby was born kind of fucked up in the head. He had a missing toe but didn't let that define his character. Scooby would take other dogs down by biting they ass and not letting go. Thug tells Tyrone they can steal some puppies from Pookie's trap in the hood.

"Pookie fight his dogs for $5 to $10g's. He be betting on them fights, they bloodline going eat some shit up."

"And what! Get ate straight the fuck up." Tyrone don't wanna go by those dogs. Thug tells Tyrone about the cracka on the North Side who has pits.

Tyrone asks how big the mama dog is and where she at. Thug told him she don't bite, that bitch a straight shit eater. "Puppies can go for the hun dun."

Floesha was home looking through the Pineburg Times Newspaper. She wasn't interested in reading any sorts of stories, and she didn't have any kin who died. That hoe was targeting families in the obituary, plotting to do a BNE. She breaks into people's houses and steals their shit while they are at wakes and funerals. Floesha is ghetto as fuck! You can't get any ghettoer than this. And Tyrone doesn't fall too far from the tree. She's on her third house. She borrowed one of her nigga's cars, and it was his girlfriends. She knows how to play the game just like these niggas.

Floesha calls her home girl, Tawanna who steals clothes with her. She needs her to drive on the lick. She picks her up, and they drive by and see the house unoccupied. It's in a neighborhood crime watch community. Floesha checks for any alarm signs and once everything was clear, she backs the car into the drive way and get out.

Tawanna gets in the drivers seat with the engine running, ready to haul ass. Flo knocks on the front door like she stays there and rings the doorbell. No one answers. No dogs running to the front door means no dogs inside. So, she goes to the back of the house to check to see if there's any dogs behind the gate. She makes sure the neighbors don't have any doors or windows open or worse, walk out to fuck up the lick. The coast is clear, so Flo breaks open the back window of the house. She took Tyrone's flat head screw driver to get in. Floesha climbs through the window falls and hits her collar bone on the counter of the bathroom sink. She gets up and search each bedroom for valuables.

When she was done, Floesha checks all the windows to make sure no one would see her coming out. A neighbor had seen her through the back glass sliding door. He was in his back yard on the phone with the police. Floesha noticed him looking an hit it through the front door and hopped in the car. Tawanna got the fuck from around there. The place was ransacked. They drove to Mercy Hospital shortly after the break in. Floesha had a sharp pain in her left shoulder. She chipped her collar bone tumbling through the window. Karma!

Ms. White calls the attendance. "Good morning, children.

Good morning Ms. White."

Ms. White smiles, "I'll be calling attendance to make sure everyone is here.

Just say here and raise your hand."

"Bob Brett."

"Here."

"Sarah Lynn."

"Here."

"Tanner Brody."

"Here."

"Cove Colton."

"Here."

"Jocqueta Jenkins," There was a moment of silence.

"Jocqueta Jenkins."

Jocqueta was there, but she was too embarrassed to answer the teacher because her name sounded different than the other students.

It's her first day at Pinecone Elementary, an all-white school. Jocqueta Jenkins raises here hand slowly. The class starts laughing. Johnny the jokester yell out loud to the class, "Everybody, Jocqueta ain't got no drawers on." Jocqueta mean mug 'em. "Ya mammy. I bet i know how to fight doe."

Johnny get quiet. She told the white boy she going rob him for his lunch money and she want it all before snack time. Including his snacks. Jocqueta was a 7 year old bully.

Tyrone and his friends ride their bikes to buddy Sarah's house. They need to borrow her car to go to the mall to steal some shoes. All four of them drive to the mall in Sarah's car. It's like she lives in the MOTHAFUCKA with her clothes and trash in the seat! Someone had to stay with the car. It was on Bre this time to be the driver.

He parks by the nearest exit with the engine running for a quick getaway.

Tyrone, Lil Nick, and Thug all go inside. They walk around first to locate all the mall security guards. On their way to the shoe store, Tyrone has to go to the bathroom to take a nervous shit. Every time they do something bad, he always has to take a shit first.

After he is done, the three boys go into the shoe store and start asking about the shoes they have and the sizes. While the lady helps Nick and Thug, Tyrone asks for other shoes he likes in a 7 1/2 in all black. The male employee tells him they only have what's on the shelf.

"They don't have them in black?"

The employee goes to the back and brings Tyrone a box of shoes. He actually gives Tyrone both pairs to try on. While Tyrone tries his shoes on, Lil Nick is telling the lady the shoes he wants. She goes to the back and brings the shoes to the counter. Tyrone has his new shoes on, pacing back and forth. Thug is talking to the male employee like nothing is fixing to happen, trying to keep him from asking Tyrone questions about paying. The female employee brings the 2nd pair of shoes to the register for both boys. They act like they are getting money out when Tyrone first takes off running.

At the same time, Nick and Thug each grab a shoe box off the counter and run like hell. Right behind Tyrone, through the mall, they bust out the exit door and jump in the car's back and front seat. Bre, the getaway driver, takes off and asks them if they got him anything. They all said no.

"We didn't have time," said Nick.

"Next time, someone else is staying in the car," Bre said.

The three boys couldn't even talk yet, since their hearts were racing and adrenaline pumping. They all head to Thugga's house to sort shit out.

Thugga has a big stash of everybody's clothes at his house. So they all went through and traded clothes around until everyone was happy with what they wearing. Everyone except Bre had brand new shoes, but he was alright. Some took showers and some didn't. They all just hang out at Thug's house before they get ready to go out. Thug's mama is cool. She treats all his friends like her own children and didn't care if they come to her house even if he wasn't there. It's time to go and everyone's fresh. They still have buddy, Sarah's car. Bre wants to take highway I-275 where you can see the top of the baseball stadium. He juice it on the ramp while smoking weed and swerving in and out of traffic. Bre was stunting so hard he got out of the car in the middle of the highway and takes a picture standing in front of the car. He jumps back in, flushed it and post it on social media. That nigga is hilarious.

The buddy's whip was so dogged out and damaged, they didn't give a fuck about it. Ashes and gar guts all on the seat. Weed all in the center console. The car got them from point A to point B, so they can't complain. Tyrone's phone rings, but he won't answer. He knows who it is and sends her to his voice mail.

"Hello, T-man. I need my car! I have to pick up my daughter! Can you please pick up the phone? That wasn't enough you gave me. And it was garbage! I didn't get high! I need another hit," said Sarah.

They pull up to Club Exclusive. It was swole as hell. The parking lot was completely full, and Bre barely found a spot to park. Tyrone and Nick are strapped with guns but left them in the car. Jax performing so his fans come out to show love. He was a local rapper from the city. They all get out and post up outside for a minute so they can see who all coming in. Security was tight and trying to get people inside so it's not packed outside. Everyone makes their way in. It's dark. The music is loud and security doesn't seem to care about a bitch smoking weed inside, as long as they stay inside with it.

Everyone moving around and throwing up their hoods. There were songs for the dope boys, jack boys, fuck boys, and slow songs for the babes. Jax was the opening act. Tyrone and his homeboys are all posted in a pack. Tyrone got a couple of dances from some girls and their numbers. One girl told him his breath smell like a wet dog. He forgot to bring chewing gum. Nick belt pops from a girl shaking that ass so fast on him. Thug and Bre don't dance.

When it was time for Jax to perform, He walks out with his niggas. Dj Coop play his record and Jax do his thang on stage. Jax straight snap he can rap. The picture man was charging $5 for a picture taken and $10 with the rapper. Some jits wanted to bump each other in the club and got put out while Jax was performing. He came on stage 30 minutes before midnight. After his show, Dj Coop put the music back in rotation.

Exclusive lit. When it was over everybody start posting outside the club.

Tyrone and his home boys post in front of the building trying to holler at hoes. The club was always super packed after 2:00 am. That's when the most shit happens and niggas come to hang out. The police are always there to make sure these kids go home. But there is too many people to keep up with. A fight breaks out in the crowd. It's two hoes fighting over a nigga name Zaddy.

Zaddy ain't shit either. He don't even want to break up the fight. He letting them hoes fight. The police make their way through the crowd and pepper spray the girls until they stop fighting. Just as the police calm things down and arrest the two, a fight breaks out across the parking lot. Gun shots ring out. Somebody's busting!

Everybody starts running in every direction. The police head towards the shots. Tyrone and his home boys hit it because they have guns, and no one has a license to drive. They are all too young. So, they head back to the hood. Tyrone has the wheel. The buddy's car was so fucked up it had no gas, and nobody wanted to put gas in the tank. Not even $2 dollars.

They felt the car was through anyway and nobody wanted to take full responsibility for the damages. Tyrone drives the car to a vacant house and left the engine running. Lil Nick put a brick on the gas pedal, and it starts to make grooves in the dirt with leaves flying everywhere. The engine eventually caught fire, burning half of the house. They walk to the neighborhood park rolling up, laughing about what they just did.

"Sarah better tell the police a bitch stole her shit," said Tyrone. They pull an all-nighter. Everyone went home when the sun was coming up.

Tyrone and Thug skip school to go steal some pit bull puppies from a white guy. Thug knows his schedule and what time he leaves. The cracka leave at 8. They rode their bikes there, put 'em, down and scaled the fence to see if the puppies were in the yard. And they were. The mama dog was in the window wagging her tail. The puppies are around 5 months old and raw. They jump the fence and each grab a dog and ride back to the hood. The white guy have them on camera with shirts over their face looking stupid. Pappy, an OG, him and his sons are riding with ski masks on in Tyrone's neighborhood.

They are looking for the boys who pistol-whipped and stole their daddy's car. They drive to the old car wash and sit for a minute to see if Pappy sees anyone familiar. They sit for a while, and he hasn't recognized anyone. Pappy was one of the originals who brought large quantities of dope in Pineburg back in the days. He has family all over town. And they stick together. They don't play. Everyone knows the Dunbar family and how they get down. You fight one brother, you fight all the brothers - no one on ones.

There was a time in the city when Pappy rose to prominence in the game. He had the streets feared and on lock. But all that jail time got to his head. Pappy wasn't the same person when he got out. He lost his mind a little and went kind of crazy. Pappy had 20 kids. His children are heavy in the game. They are the Dunbar family, aka "The Highland Boys." Pappy has a son name Soulja. He's a robber from Sun Peak Projects, the old projects, before they were rebuilt. Soulja shot people and been shot. He's been through the battlefield. People know what's up with him.

Soulja had robber friends. Mud, Keno, and Boo Man were notorious robbers. One minute they play cards with you, the next minute they robbing you and the entire card table. Soulja's baby mama doesn't want anything to do with him because their house got shot up one time. They have a kid and she doesn't want to be around that kind of lifestyle. Soulja is a real soldier. His older brother was Poppa. Poppa that nigga. He's the brick man. The brothers been flipping bricks since they were teenagers.

Pappy taught his 20 kids the game. Some of his sons put big rims on dope boy cars. Others rode low key, dark tent, and a couple drove regular cars that were in school. Poppa got money setting up spots. Cousin Pookie is his right hand man.

Poppa made money off of Pookie fronting him drugs. Pookie told 'em, about the niggas who did that to his daddy. Poppa has a lot of lil niggas that's about that life. He calls them his shooters. They stay cross town and are known as Cross. A bunch of jits who Poppa put on in his spots. They'll do anything for him. He has all types of family and friends that love him.

Pineburg Police Department had history with the Dunbar family. The chief's dad, Keith Scott Sr. was a former chief who was responsible for bringing down Pappy Dunbar. He was there the last night Pappy could terrorize the streets. Following in his dad's footsteps, his son, Chief Keith Scott Jr. wanted to keep law enforcement in his bloodline. So, he became a police officer like his dad.

Keith was only selected chief because of who his dad was. Chief Keith would target black kids in lower income neighborhoods. He is a major asshole in inner city policing. The chief busted associates connected to the Dunbar family. The Dunbar family was once the biggest drug dealers in Pineburg when crack first hit. Officer James "Trigg" Culberson is a trigger happy police officer. He was given that nick name throughout the black community. Trigg works in the Vice and Narcotics Division. Evan Gonzalez, aka Rambo works in vice. Rambo would catch people in the hood and beat they ass. Rambo was excessive.

He would do it when there was no one looking. Niggas called Evan, Rambo, only because what he was known to do. Steve was a narc. He ran track back in the days. People call him Superman because he's so fast. No one has out ran him yet. He always catches them. These 3 narcotic officers are super crooked. Some police officers come to work and do their job without attitude. Officer Carvin was nicknamed O.C from the kids at Pineburg Middle School.

He is a school resource officer and a part time police officer. He was one of the few good ones kids felt they could come talk to in the black community. O.C took the time to build a relationship with the children, until you broke the law, then it was time for you to go to jail.

Uncle Tom and Nephew Tommy were K9 handlers. They are nephew and uncle. Uncle Tom's sister named, Nephew Tommy after him. They're black but follow every order and act worse than the white man. They treat niggas any kind of way, going against their own. They were puppets. The Chief of Police,

Keith Scott, and his team created an operation responsible for dismantling the Dunbar family. It was called Operation Take Down. The police held briefings about the crime family and their associates. Pineburg Police's main interest was the Dunbars and grand thefts in the community. Which was at an all time high.

Tyrone, Lil Nick, Bre, and Thug need to hit a lick. These boys are on some hot boy shit, all the time can't tell them anything. They do what they want. The block has been dead, so they haven't been out. A baser told Tyrone some niggas in ski masks with golds been riding around the hood a lot, asking questions. They are older cats.

So, Tyrone and his homeboys have been laying low. They are in need of some money. The money they made off the puppies wasn't enough. Tyrone was all about getting quick cash. He would sell you his mama if he had a choice. Tyrone and his homeboys plan to do a home invasion. They want to rob Pookie and the trap since it's the closest. Cousin Pookie is a big time drug dealer who has a spot in Tyrone's neighborhood. Everybody wants to be cousins with Pookie, even if they didn't know him personally. Bitches was always saying, "THAT'S MY COUSIN!"

Pookie must have a lot of cousins. Pookie trap house sell crack cocaine. He has a mechanic at his spot to throw the police off from all that drug dealing he been doing. One of the people in his circle was Fatty. He put Fatty in the spot. Pookie got that sack being around Poppa. Them 2 look like money standing next to eachother. Tyrone and his homeboys go to Thug's house. They all want to rob Pookie's crack spot. It swings his house is in Buddy Central. The mechanic smokes crack too. The boys start planning the robbery on what they going do and how they going run in the house. The only way to get inside is through the front. Pookie has dogs in the back. It might turn to a shoot out trying to take them niggas shit. Tyrone rather just wait and do a little bit of homework first. He doesn't want to go on a suicide mission. Pookie has a studio in the spot and Tyrone and his boys record there. They have to be extra careful.

Pookie had a lot of people record there. Tyrone, Nick, Thug, and Bre decide to ride by slow, watching Pookie's spot, trying to learn more about times and people who be there. They want to know how they move. They switch cars and park down the street from Pookie's spot. They smoke in dark tent, trying to stay low-key and blend with traffic.

Abraham Park is flaming. The police stay riding through. Tyrone, Nick, Bre, and Thug come to the park at night to hang out. They always sit at the picnic tables or shoot hoops. They found a paint bucket inside an abandoned house and took it to the park. They all wrote their names on the pavement at the park - Thug, T-man, Bre, and Nick Big. Thug had gotten them a lick for 80 racks. It's in P Park at a drug dealer's house. Bre wants to go in the house. Thug wanna start a gang and call it Flame Gang Chicken Wing Flame. Thug and Bre were the Flame Gang. They wore green bandanas and all black clothes with gloves. Those two were together all the time. They were a clique inside a clique.

They came up with their slogan "Gumball Flame and Chicken Wing Flame." They straight flaming shit. Tyrone and Nick were doing their homework on Pookie's trap still. They know it's in their studio equipment, drugs, and money. They'll hit if they go in, at least that's what they think. And Pookie's got it. But they aren't trying to go front row to the murder show. Tyrone doesn't have enough man power for Pookie. So, Tyrone come up with a plan to rob the weed man. He knows him.

"He always carries a pound in a back pack." Nick with it.

"We have to use a different number."

"He'll know it's me and probably won't answer late," said Tyrone.

Tyrone and Nick leave the court while Thug and Bre stay and play basketball. Tyrone wants to hit tonight. Tyrone calls one of his dawgs, Speedy and puts him on game. Speedy don't give a fuck. He a jit out the bricks. The weed man is Gary, Scary La Gary. Speedy calls Gary and Gary answers.

"Hello? Who dis?"

"I need an ounce and an 8th."

"Who dis and how did you get my number?"

"From Dread."

He makes up a name of how he got his number without telling his name. Gary told him he was going to meet him in 20 minutes.

Track 3

Risk It 4 The Biscuit

Tyrone, Lil Nick, and Speedy ride bikes to meet Gary, a petty hustler. He didn't carry a gun, and Tyrone them knew it. He's a quick and easy lick. Tyrone rides to baser Katie's house. Katie doesn't know what's going on. She has a gate around her house so no one can see shit. They just need somebody location.

They go inside the gate and sit and wait on Gary. Twenty minutes later, Speedy calls Gary back to see where he's at. He's late. Gary told 'em, he was pulling up now. Gary pulls up with a back pack on, and of course, no gun. He rode a bike. Gary calls Speedy and tells him he's in the back alley. Speedy told him to come through the back gate. Speedy meets Gary in the back.

Tyrone and Nick are out of sight, out of mind. Speedy wants to check it out before he buys it and Gary hands him a small nugget out the bag to smell. Scary La Gary don't want jit to cuff any weed. Speedy smells it and asks to see the rest. While Gary's eyes are glued to where that nugget is going, Speedy is hoping he forgets. Gary is on that scary ass shit! Speedy snatch it out his hand and run. He didn't know, jit fast. Tyrone and Nick come from Gary's blind side and draw down on him with shirts over their faces like the Taliban.

"You already know what it is." Gary put up his hands, "A stick up!"

Lil Nick snatch the back pack he have and searches through it. They search his pants for more stuff to take. They rob Gary for everything he had with him. They even took his bike and sent him home walking. They all left after and went to Tyrone's house in the hood.

They get to his crib and dump the bag out. Gary had a QP of loud, an ounce of mid, a scale, baggies, and $200 in cash. Tyrone and Nick broke down and split the QP. They only gave Speedy $100 and a half of mid. Tyrone and Nick split the rest. They got off really using Speedy's face. Nick stays at Tyrone's house, and they slept in the car.

They wake up and go in Tyrone's house. The boys slept for the first half of the day when they were supposed to be in school. They stayed up all night smoking. Late afternoon, they get up and go outside. Tyrone and Nick roll a joint an smoke in the broken down car. It smells stale as a MOTHAFUCKA! Tyrone fucking up Nick education. He's becoming a terrible influence following behind Tyrone. Nick is a part of the hood now. They share clothes and wear the same shit for days, nuts stank as hell.

Thug and Bre already scoped the place. They know the times Fatty leaves his house. They go in and will leave nothing unturned. They will flip everything. He was Thug's lick. He got put on Fatty by a middle man name June. All June wanted was to get broke off. Thug didn't wanna go alone. He wants Bre to watch his back.

So, June tells Thug there's $80 racks in the house. June wants $50,000 and Thug will keep $30,000 since he's putting him on. Thug's a young nigga that's hungry so he takes it. June knows Fatty. He's been to his house before. So he wants to back door the man and go in his shit. June is a snake in disguise that can't be trusted.

Fatty stays in Pinecone Park. Thug and Nick are waiting on Fatty to leave his baby momma's house early morning. The house was ducked off on a cul-de-sac. They have a time they are going in. They are hiding on the side of Fatty's house and it's raining. They see Fatty and his baby momma backing out of the driveway. They are going to Fatty's baby momma's salon. Fatty drives off to the salon. After he drops his baby momma and kids off, he heads to the trap. Thug and Bre break in Fatty's house through the side door to the garage. They had to kick the inside door in to get inside the house. Fatty has a car on rims in the garage.

Thug starts in the living room flipping the couches over, checking the seats and ripping the bottom of the couch to see if anything was inside the couch, but he found nothing. He checks inside the kitchen cabinets, refrigerator, and washing machine. People would hide their money anywhere. Bre is searching the bedrooms under the mattress. That's where he finds 3 hand guns. He checks the dirty clothes basket and looks in the closet where he sees tons of clothes that came out the cleaners and shoes.

They have flat screens bolted to the wall. But the only thing they came for was the money. Thug calls June about where the money might be. June told Thug to look in the bottom of the stove for the money. Thug runs back in the kitchen and pulls out the stove drawer and finds $80,000 in cash. Thug runs and tells Bre. Bre runs back excited. They put all the money inside a pillow case. They kept searching the house for about 8 minutes. Their adrenaline was rushing. They ran back to the car. The neighbors couldn't see anything because it was raining so hard. Them niggas did that.

They go back to Thugga's house where they met June. June got $50,000 and Thug got $30,000. Thug gave Bre $15 grand out the money. June know he got off decent without doing anything. Thug and Bre kept the straps.

Daryll's Pajama Party from 9pm-2am @ 2044 Pine Blvd Sept 12. Leave the drama at yo' mama house BYOB hosted by Tawanna the realist bit$h. Daryll was a party promoter who all the hoes knew. Everybody know them hoes be at Daryll's parties. Daryll was flamboyant like hell. Heyyy!

He threw just about every party he could think of. Daryll's Wipe Me Down Party, Daryll's Beach Party, Daryll's Going Away Party, Daryll's Welcome Home Party, even a Darryll's Black and White Party. Daryll posts the flyer on his social media pages.

The chief of police held a briefing with the Pineburg Police Department. The Vice and Narcotics Division have been investigating a drug house for several months on Highland. Vice Squad Officer Trigg is trying to execute a search warrant from the judge. He knows the location is a drug house. He submits his affidavit to Judge Federico. Legend has it Federico once made a bet with another judge on who would be the first to give out a million years to black people. It was for a Penny at a Tea Party. The rumor circulated from the jail house only amongst the inmates.

Trigg wants them shut down. Superman and Rambo know the Dunbar family get their cars fixed there. That's how the police associate the two.

That's how they found out about Pookie's drug activity. O.C, and the Patrol Division were in another briefing in a different room about the crime rate. Auto thefts by teens are at an all-time high.

It's becoming an epidemic. There's a war being fought with these juveniles constantly. Snacs to Crac has had the most vehicle thefts. There's always kids hanging out and selling drugs there. They don't give a damn about the loitering sign. They would even go as far as asking you for 50 cent. The police wonder if the store owner is allowing these kids to be there. Half the arrests at the store the police try to get the owner to trespass them and he won't because the kids be paying him off.

Judge Federico didn't issue a search warrant because he felt there wasn't enough evidence presented to get the house searched. He inform Trigg that if he mysteriously happens to find a crumb of crack in his yard then it's a differen't scenario. Trigg and the vice squad run Pineburg. Pineburg is their city with or without the judge's consent. Pineburg Police Department do what they want. They are the law. Trigg wants to raid the property with a fake no knock warrant. The vice squad unit will go along with the drug bust on Trigg's commands.

Pineburg Police executed a date to raid the house and arrest the subjects. Superman and Rambo went out and got individuals' names from the residents, and they all have records that show cocaine charges, possession of cocaine with the intent to sell, prostitution, and petty thefts. Everybody in the house had drug charges on their records.

Fatty found out who went into his house and the streets always talk. Fatty got word that June had something to do with it. He's been flashing wads of cash on social media ever since the break in. Bragging he got this and that to them hoes when he was just broke. So, he paid niggas to kidnap him. He sent them to Junes house to get 'em.

They trick June. Fatty calls June on 3 way and tells him he wants him to check out some drugs. He said he was outside in the front of his house. So, June comes out the door and walks up to the car.

It's an ambush Fatty's goons pull guns on him out the backseat. They order him to get in the car. June is scared as hell and gets in. The goons drive him back to a secluded location and torture him to get information from him. They were beating and pistol-whipping June, and just as they were going to light him on fire, he gave in. He tells them Thugga, who be at Abraham Park, is the one who went in your house.

The goons take June back to his house and get the rest of Fatty's money and rob June. He is lucky to be alive. They are killers. It's been a couple days and Fatty already has the names of who broke into his house. Fatty calls one of his homeboys to ask about Thug and Abraham Park. Fatty put a hit on Thug's head for $30 bands. The streets ain't been safe for none of them. Tyrone, Thug, Nick, and Bre have been hanging out at baser Sam's house. She lives in the hood. Shit has been hot lately. Big niggas with money looking for them young niggas.

Fatty's cousin found out where Tyrone be at and he knows Thug and him hang together. Fatty's cousin comes to baser Sam's house unannounced with someone in a black SUV. He got a shirt over a submachine gun sweating. He comes in while Tyrone and Nick were in the living room. Fatty's cousin was trying to intimidate Tyrone. He told Tyrone he heard he got something to do with his cousin's house getting broke into i'll kill you right now. Just to get a little information out of him. Tyrone was so scared, he said thug had something to do with his house getting broke into. Tyrone even told him where Thug stay at. Nick didn't say anything. He kept quiet on the couch. Bre was in the back room and could hear Tyrone telling on who broke into Fatty's house and where they live.

Bre thought that was some flaw ass shit what Tyrone just did. He didn't say anything about it, but he just knew Tyrone wasn't right. Thug knows everywhere he goes he has to be strapped. He is trying to be as low key as possible, He is a moving target. Niggas want his head. So instead of being in the hood, he has been at his auntie house for a while. Sometimes, he takes hot boy chances and will ride a bike back crosstown. The Dunbar family be on Highland in a yard.

It's Poppa's spot. His dad would come by to cook up that yellow 80's dope once a while. He still had it in him a little and remembered how to work the stove. Poppa is the man. He sold pounds of mid and loud. He also has a mean wrist game cooking dope. Poppa runs the neighborhood, and he got the Cross jits on point. He's big homie to them.

Poppa's shooter, Trap Monkey is in the trap. He doesn't have anywhere to stay besides the trap. His people kicked him out. Trap Monkey was a trigger happy young jit. Poppa lets Trap Monkey know about Tyrone. So now, Cross wanna do something to Tyrone. They're doing it out of respect. Poppa wants Tyrone dead. Cross plan on coming through the cut at night in Tyrone's neighborhood and shooting at him. They gone try to get 'em, one way or the other.

It was said that Pappy had a complicated machine in his house back in the days that sold drugs at specific times. The neighborhood went inside the house at certain times because they were too afraid of the shootings. Pappy terrorized the community and made a name for himself. Pappy Boys! They didn't want anything to do with him and was too terrified to report it to the authorities. When Pappy got arrested, they cheered he was going away. This was in the 80's.

Pappy Dunbar's sons are on a man hunt looking for Tyrone. Trap Monkey and his friends Lil' D and Nut get a rental and some guns and go through Tyrone's neighborhood. The Cross jits drive where they see Tyrone and his friends standing in front of Mr. Jake's house.

They speed through and go back to their neighborhood on that creep shit. Cross drive back when it gets dark and ride through again. Tyrone and everybody are still in front of Mr. Jake's house. Trap Monkey got the wheels, so he parks the car a street over. All 3 boys run through the cut and up guns on Tyrone, Nick, Cortez, and Josh and start shooting. Tyrone them ran so fast up out of there. He didn't have a gun on him. Josh have a gun he borrowed but didn't even shoot back. Cortez's house almost got shot. It was grazed by a bullet.

The Cross jits ran back to their car and smashes off. Tyrone and his friends were heated, wondering who the fuck just shot at them. Tyrone takes the pistol from Josh and told him he doesn't need a gun if he isn't going to shoot. Josh was acting like he was going to shoot after the fact. Tyrone and his friends have been beefing with people in the city. Someone called the police since the shooting was next to houses. By the time the police arrive, everybody was gone.

The police start looking for shell casings on the ground after they rope the area off. The block is even hotter. Tyrone and a few of them went to his house. Of course, Floesha came out cussing at Tyrone and all his friends about standing in front of her house. Cortez went back inside to find his sister, nieces, and nephews scared to death. Cortez's sister yelling.

"I don't want people standing in front of my house, especially bringing trouble. It's not their house so they don't care." Cortez is snapping he got a small ass revolver from inside ready for anyone to come back to his people's house. No one comes back though. His house wasn't even the target. It just got caught in the middle of Tyrone's mess.

Daryll and Tawanna's Pajama Party was on smash. Daryll had the music playing really loud, not caring about what his neighbors had to say. People were standing in front of his neighbors house and blocking their drive way. Bitches were throwing trash in Daryll's yard not giving a fuck.

Tawanna, Floesha, and Daryll all had their pajamas on. Tawanna and Flo go outside telling people it's cups in the house for the low. Then she jumps in her U-Haul truck making Flo get in. Tawanna is so crunk, she turns up the music, loud funking hoe songs. She speeds up the street to the store for gars. Faggots like to drive fast. When she gets back, Tawanna steps on the gas and break burning out up the street. She did a donut in the middle of the intersection so everyone can see then pulls up real fast. "Faggot ass someone shouted in the crowd."

Floesha gets out, fuck nigga this pussy nigga that. Smoking a black. She wet going back and forth with everybody and they mama. Floesha needed to go home. Tawanna arguing with a nigga she barely know ready to fight. She gets a good look at him and exposes his undercover, wanna be dope boy ass. The crowd laughs at their awkward dispute. He gets mad and runs up on Tawanna with his set up. Tawanna is still a nigga no matter what you wanna call it.

Tawanna drop the girl act and starts throwing blows right away. They fighting by the cars. She grabs the boys dreads, hit him in the face and push him against someone else's car. They put a dent in it. Now that person threatening to whoop both their asses if they don't pay up. Tawanna wrestles with the guy onto the ground. Tawanna jumps on top of the guy pounding his face to the cement. Everyone at the party is watching and laughing, saying he is getting beat up by a faggot recording it. Someone had to stop the fight and pull Tawanna off the guy it got so bad. They thought he was about dead and that he has aids now getting Tawanna blood on him.

The nigga was trying to cop deuces after that ass whooping trying to shake Tawanna hand talking about bet that up bro. The outside of Daryll's house was thick. Everybody was riding through. The street got so packed, no one could hardly move their car.

The Peckerwood family hears a helicopter hovering over their house early Sunday morning. Linda Peckerwood, the mom, steps outside to see what's going on. She sees a group of teens running from the police.

Track 4

The Peckerwoods

Tyrone and his friends are in hot wheels. They drive a stolo down the Peckerwoods road. Linda was hoping those thugs get caught. She goes back inside and continue watching the morning news. Where an 11 year old boy who just got out robbed a burger joint with a pocket knife.

"Where he's going his buns will be the only thing roasting," said Linda.

Linda cooks breakfast on a bad eye that has to be replaced.

That eye smells like something is burning. Her husband, Robert comes out the bedroom, dick hard from watching interracial porn. His wife barely gives him any, and it's boring when she does. Every time she does, it's on her side. They've been fucking in that same position for years. Robert trips the next day. It never fails. It's like he wakes up with an attitude and finds a reason to flip out. Robert went into the kitchen mad. He just jacked off and felt guilty afterwards about the waste of a nut. First thing Robert sees on the window frame is burnt cigarette marks. He flips the fuck out. Robert always has to tell Linda about putting her ashes in the window. Their son Shawn, who is 14, was getting out of the shower without drying off entirely. Water is all on the bathroom floor, and he never cleans up behind himself. Shawn leaves his clothes behind the bathroom door constantly.

Linda always has to tell Shawn about doing that. Shawn goes into the kitchen drying off and puts his wet towel on the back of the chair. Just leaving it anywhere. Shit like that gets on Linda nerves. She gets on him. Linda's mad, Robert's mad, and now Shawn's mad. The devil is alive in the Peckerwoods threshold. Shawn doesn't want to eat. Now he thinks he's hurting his mom, but he's not. He wants to be an ass hole if it ain't about him.

Linda and Rob eat, sleep, and breath church. Shawn was tired of that shit. It's long and boring as hell so he usually falls asleep. He doesn't want to go. They make him go all the time so he would rather give his mom a hard time about going. Robert tells Shawn, "You don't have a choice. You are going to church." Shawn tells his dad "He has a choice." Robert forces Shawn to go to church. Robert had a problem checking the doors twice when he left the house.

The Peckerwoods are all in the car. Linda is driving, so she starts the engine and backs out of their drive way onto the road. A car was coming and almost crashes into them. She has to slam on her brakes, giving her a little jerk. The other car blew their horn. That infuriates Linda. Her face instantly turns red. She backs out of the drive way so fast and speeds off after the car. The car comes to a stop at the stop sign. So, Linda pulls up next to them and rolls her window down. She gives them the finger and says, "What the fuck? Can you fucking drive asshole?"

She then cuts the other car off, speeding and heated. Linda drives like a crazy ass lunatic the rest of the way to church. Shawn asks his mom if she can slow the fuck down and drive like a christian.

She was scaring the kids. There is a speed trap by the church, and Linda got pulled into the parking lot of Church of Hill for speeding. Linda Peckerwood cries and lies to the officer and told him she didn't know her license was suspended. He let her go with a warning.

The Peckerwoods walk into the church building. There are bishops and ministers greeting all of the families entering. Everyone comes in and finds a seat, waiting for the pope to start his Sunday morning service. The Peckerwoods made everyone think they were the perfect little family. Before the pope preaches, one of his deacons comes up to collect the weekly tithes. The pope was charging people for his service. A thousand dollars was his starting bid. And if you didn't have that, hell, he would take $250. And if you still don't have that amount, there is an ATM machine by all the exits, "Oh! Uh-Uh!" One of the people blurt out.

As he blesses there helpful pocket books, Brother Deacon Jones passes the collection plate to go around the church. Members and visitors start putting money in it. Linda's light bill was high, so she blames the devil for her dealings, and steals money out the collection plate. People are going to the ATM machine. After the church pays its tithes, the pastor walks to the podium and starts to talk.

He introduces himself as Pastor Pope John Fathers III. He got people to believe he is the closest thing to god. He starts preaching and Shawn is somewhere in outer space. He started looking for church hotties, but there isn't any, so now he's really bored and feels there's no point in going. Pastor Pope John has been preaching for an hour, when a man gets out of his seat and yells at the pastor. He tells the pastor he's the devil, stealing money from the people of the church and community.

He turns to the people and tells them the pastor has gotten very wealthy off their money, and he lives in a big house on Golden Street. "Golden Street is where the rich folks lives." He says the pastor is charging them for religion. He tells everyone the pastor drives a very expensive car. The man is so mad, he charges at the pastor, but the people stop him in his tracks and carries him away. The pastor was yelling back, "I'm not robbing anyone." After a minute, the crowd calms down and the pastor tells everyone that man forgot to take his medication this morning. "He's a little bit crazy," and continues on with the word. Church was over.

The Peckerwood family all got into a small car and left church. Robert is a neighborhood crime watch captain. He really thinks he's the police. He carries his gun and permit everywhere he goes, even in church ready to stand his ground. There will be a neighborhood crime watch meeting at the community center. He wants to discuss the crime that has been going on in their neighborhood. Robert tells Linda he is tired of black people dropping trash, playing loud music at all sorts of hours in the morning and at night, and driving recklessly on his road. "Linda, I even put a 'slow down, kids at play' sign, and they hit that," he said. "I'm tired of these niggers and their nigglets. I wish they would have jumped off the boat and drowned coming to AmeriKKKa."

Shawn was in the backseat and all he could think about was selling one of his dad's guns to his weed dealer, Tyrone for some weed. Tyrone is a master manipulator. Shawn was a real weed head. When they pull up to their house, the black family across from

52

them were having a family gathering. There were tons of cars parked in their yard and on the road. Since their cars weren't parked correctly, it outraged Linda. She said there were cars blocking her driveway and in her yard. But really, no one was on her property line. When Linda gets in her house, she calls a tow truck company to come remove her neighbors' cars. When they get there and realize that no one is blocking her driveway or parked on her property, they leave. Linda is pissed the cars are still there and calls the police.

"911 operator," said dispatch.

"White woman in distress," said Linda. I need a police officer to come to my house. My black neighbors are being hostile. When I asked them nicely to move their cars off my property, they refused. Can you please send a white officer?" Linda is always sticking her nose where it doesn't belong. She is always up someone's ass.

When the police arrive and investigate both parties, they did not find a probable cause to do anything. Instead, they told Linda there's nothing they can do, and that she needs to go in the house and mind her business. She thought the police would side with a white family first, but instead, they went with the black family. After Linda went inside, the other family went back to their gathering and Pineburg Police left. An hour goes by, and Linda felt it was in her best interest that something has to happen. So the family went across the street and Linda pours human remains on top of someone's car out of a Kool-Aid jar. There was blonde pubic hair sticking out of the turds. Then, Linda decide since they didn't want to leave, she would jam paper clips inside the key holes to the other cars so, they won't be able to open their car doors. Linda even bent a license plate out of frustration.

When the gathering was over and people started to leave, someone notices shit on top of their car, and it wasn't from a bird.

They immediately suspect the Peckerwoods and call the police. When the police shows up and starts investigating and finger printing the cars, Linda confesses. They locked her ass up wasting their time. She was charged with disorderly conduct and 5 counts of criminal damage. She was also heavily intoxicated since she started drinking after the police left the first time. She was pissed they didn't side with her.

Pineburg Police stated this wasn't the first time they had to come out to Linda's residence after she called the police on her neighbor. She called them last Christmas, a time when everybody was supposed to be happy, but Linda wasn't. It was always something with her. She will call the police about the stupidest things. It was like an on-going silent war between the two families. Linda was released from jail and her neighbors had dubbed her "Silent War Linda." Her charges were later dropped due to her using her White Privilege Card (WPC).

At the community center meeting, they talk about the new campaign. "If you see something, you say something." Robert stands up and says, "If you're tired of these so-called thugs and gangstas destroying our neighborhoods and brainwashing our children into doing evil, then stand with me. I will no longer tolerate these dread head, baggy drawers showing, standing in front of the store every time I try to go to the store, I have to go to another store because of it. Thugs terrorize our streets, our homes, and our families. Stand with me as your watch dog community captain. We must take back Pineburg. I own my home, and THESE THUGS are just paying rent."

Robert Peckerwood is sick of all the criminal activity that plagues his neighborhood. When the meeting was over, Robert drives through his neighborhood, profiling all the black kids that live there hanging on the street corners and in the middle of the road. It makes him sick to his stomach. They are all thugs to Robert, and he hates thugs. Tyrone's street is separate from Robert's by the next neighborhood over.

When Robert is done driving around profiling, he goes home. While he was pulling in his driveway, Robert sees Tyrone and a group of boys riding bicycles. Tyrone and his neighborhood friends were in all black, looking inside people's cars. Robert spots a bike that looks like his son's bike that got stolen 2 weeks ago. He wasn't going to let them get away that easy, so he speeds up to the boys and stops in front of them. He jumps out of his car and one of Tyrone's friends yell, "Run!" All but one, who didn't know what was going on, started to run. Robert punches the teen in the left eye so hard, he spins around and falls to the ground.

Robert grabs his bike throws it in his car and drives home. He left the boy lying on the side of the street with a black eye. Some of the neighborhood kids seen him in the middle of the road, so they helped him. They gave him a ride home on their handle bars. Robert gets home and realizes he took the wrong bike.

The Peckerwoods are a family of sinners posing as saints. Linda is the most racist of them all, while Robert is learning his surroundings and Shawn is adapting to them. The Peckerwood family thought they bought their house somewhere on the beach, but come to find out, it's right in the hood. So, they just deal with it. Four days after Robert punched the kid and took his bike, the Peckerwoods' house get shot up. Linda wondered who could have done such a thing. She didn't know Robert got into a confrontation the other day. They low-key hated the south.

Bad shit was always happening, and they couldn't keep anything on their porch. There grill was even stolen! A helicopter is always circling around their house. They don't do that normally in a predominately white neighborhood. Shawn is at Pineburg Middle School.

Him and some of his friends started a chain message, and Shawn wrote about having access to his dad's guns. Someone in the chain message told the teacher on him. Shawn was in deep trouble. The SWAT team came, along with the FBI. They rope the whole school off. They hand cuff and search Shawn thoroughly for a gun but didn't find any. They were talking about expelling Shawn, but his parents came in and used their White Privilege Cards to get Shawn off the hook. It's $100 renewals a year.

After getting Shawn out of school and holding him hostage for an hour and a half, they go to the gas station, Snacs to Crac. As soon as they pull up, crack heads were trying to pump their gas and get them what they need from inside. At the same time, kid dealers were asking if they were straight and calling Linda "Auntie." It was like a Zombie Apocalypse at the store. Linda yells back at one of the little boys, "Are you straight? Because I am!" They wanted to just hurry up and get the fuck out of there. Robert actually gives one of the junkies money to get them things they wanted. He was just trying to get the guy out of his face, but Linda wanted Robert to go in. He said he will get the things, so we don't have to get out the car.

Linda yells, "You dumb ass! You gave money to a crack head. And you actually think he's coming back." They sit and wait for 5 minutes, then 10 minutes, then 15. Linda is yelling at Robert. So, he gets out and tries to find the guy. He had no luck the gentlemen was long gone. Robert pumps the gas and Linda cusses him out the whole way home. Robert ignores half the things she says. He is looking at everyone's grass that is overgrown. Small things like that get to Robert.

He sees a few houses down from him and immediately calls code compliance. He leaves a message on their voicemail about how his neighbors overgrown grass is affecting the view from his front living room. It just so happens that the house he's talking about is the neighborhood lawn mans. He's known for dumping illegally in the middle of people's alleys late at night or in the early morning when nobody can see.

They pull up and as soon as they get out, 2 guys come up trying to sell them bootleg cable. Linda tells them they're not interested in illegal cable. Tyrone and his friends are driving a stolen car speeding down the Peckerwoods' street. Shawn watches them drive by flying. He secretly loves how these boys in the hood act. The dog catcher is right behind 'em, going to a police call. Pit bulls bit a black boy with dreads a couple times. The dogs also attacked the teens dog.

There was a pack of 5 attacking him and his dog that came across the street from where he lives. The lil nigga had to jump on a truck passing by to get away from them. These dogs were out for blood. They even flattened one of the guy's tires off his truck, trying to get that boy. The guy in the truck was so afraid for the young mans safety, he had to drive to the church parking lot down the street to get away from these animals. When the police arrived, they had to shoot one of the dogs for being so aggressive.

The ambulance takes him to Mercy Hospital, where an officer takes his statement about the incident. He tells them the dogs got out of his neighbor's gate and ran in his yard, attacking him when he opened the fence to his gate. His dog got out trying to help. The neighbor's dogs attacked him first and came on his property. The police department had twisted a bitch story since there was only one officer present. He wrote in his report the victim couldn't tell which dog bit him. So, they told the dog catcher to take all the dogs to the pound. Even Trons dog had to go, although it didn't do anything but curl up in a ball. Keemone, whose dogs got out and attacked Tron, found out what happened through his girlfriend brother. Who was also at the hospital at the time.

That's how the police were able to contact him. When he returned home, he lied to the police and told him Tron was trying to break into his house. That's how his dogs got out.

Everyone on the street knows Keemone dogs stay busting loose. Stuff like this only happens on the south side. In the meantime, the Peckerwoods call their dealer, Fatty for an 8 ball of cocaine. Linda and Robert are functional smokers that go to church. They will only deal with people they know. They pack for their camping trip.

The Peckerwood family is going camping at the state park that's open to the public. And it's only about an hour and a half away. Linda and Robert get their camping gear together, while Shawn was busy meeting his dealer, Tyrone. Tyrone go to the same school as him and stays in his neighborhood. Shawn wants to get high before he rides with his parents. Shawn doesn't know how to roll, so he asks Tyrone can he go to the store get 'em, a gar, and roll him a joint. He'll give him his dollar back when he get there.

Tyrone knows he's asking for too much, but jit spends money so he goes with the flow. Tyrone rolls the blunt with sticks all in it. Skimp limps. Shawn doesn't care how small the joint is. He goes home and smokes in the back of the house. Linda and Robert are packed. Robert was the last to get in the car because he was too busy making sure all the water faucets are off and windows locked. They were in the car and called on Shawn. Shawn goes out to the car and gets in. His mom turns around and asks him if he has everything.

She notices a brown substance on his lips and teeth. She asks him what's that stuff on your lips. Shawn licks his teeth and doesn't say anything. It was from wetting the weed too much when he hit it. Robert double checks the house again to make sure all the doors are locked and Linda drives off to the state park. Shawn ate all of his fundraiser candy he was supposed to sell for school. When the Peckerwoods pull in, they went to find a campsite where the families are. Robert, Linda, and Shawn all get out their gear and start setting up camp.

They want to hurry and set up so they can get out and go adventuring in the park. Shawn unpacked all his things in his tent and was waiting on his parents, when he saw a girl nearby that he thought was pretty. She caught his attention. He was thinking maybe she would make his trip a little less boring. Shawn walks over to her and introduces himself. He thinks she likes him just because they are talking to each other. She's one of those friendly white girls that'll say hi to anybody. They talk, and Shawn walks back to his campsite to check and see what's taking his parents so long.

When Shawn was talking to the girl, his dad saw and thought him and Linda had time for a quickie. Shawn walks up to the site and starts calling for his mom and dad. They answer him from the tent saying, "One minute." Shawn's not stupid. He knows what's going on. His dad comes out first asking who wants to go fishing. They walk down a trail in the woods for about 20 minutes and find a nice spot to set up for the day. They were right beside a stream.

Robert, Shawn, and Linda get their fishing poles ready and start fishing. Robert grew up fishing. He knew how to catch a fish. Shawn, on the other hand, could not fish. His first cast, he wheel back in too fast. He hooks Robert's ear on the second attempt. Linda was drinking, so she lost it and was laughing at his ass. Shawn never did catch anything on his 8th cast. He gave up and threw his pole in the water. Robert made him jump in and get it.

Since he didn't know how to fish, the only thing that brought him excitement was cutting the eye balls out the fish his dad caught.

He threw them back in the water and watch them swim unbalanced, knocking into rocks. Shawn pokes their eyes out with a fork. He was being cruel for no reason. Shawn was complaining about being bored. It was time to go back to camp, so they pack up their fishing gear and left. When they get back, Linda starts gathering sticks and twigs for a fire.

Shawn wanders off on his own and stumbles on a berry bush that looks sweet to eat. So, he starts picking them off the bushes and eating them by the handful. He took some back and shared with his dad. They love them. Linda cooks dinner over a fire she built.

They all sat around the fire, and shortly after, Shawn bent over saying his stomach starting to mess up.

As soon as he stood up, he knew it was going to come out watery. One small fart and it was over. Robert has been farting constantly. His stomach started hurting, and he realized he had to shit. The bathhouse where the toilet was located was a quarter mile away. They both take off running, ass holes about to explode. Robert made it to the bathroom before Shawn. Shawn takes a shit outside. Robert sat on the toilet, sweating, twisting, turning, and wishing he was dead. He didn't want to think about anything else. Robert block everything out his mind. It made him hate the color brown because it was the color of his shit.

Robert was throwing up and cramping. He thought it was a small demon moving around in his stomach. While Shawn has his pants down and shitting outside. He takes his shirt off and wipes his booty cheeks. That shirt made his ass hole kind of itchy, so he starts scratching it with his fingers and green shit gets under his nails. Robert comes outside the bathhouse and Shawn is waiting on him.

They start walking back to camp, and Shawn was talking an pointing by his dad's face. When Robert got a whiff of what Shawn fingers smell like, he tells him his fingers smells like booty. When they get back to camp, Linda is ready to go play softball.

Anyone that comes can play. Shawn was happy. He wants to look for that girl he met earlier. They get to the field, and Shawn sees her and goes over. He tells her how pretty she is and asks if she would be his girlfriend. She tells him she just wants to be friends because she likes a older boy name Chester. "Chester the molester," said Shawn. He gets so mad and DDT the girl onto the ground.

She is crying, gets up and tells her dad what happened. He comes over and threatens to kick his ass and his parents' asses if he comes near his daughter again. Robert brandishes his gun to the guy. The man told his family, "Let's go! It's time to go!" They went back to their campsite. Meanwhile, while the Peckerwoods were out of town, the neighborhood kids are in their yard stealing mangos. Everyone calls their yard mango heaven because there's a lot of mango trees in the area. The Peckerwoods go back to their camp site to find their belongings ransacked and little paw prints by the culprit that led to the cooler. All their other stuff gone. "Raccoons!" It struck a nerve deep within Robert. He was ready to use deadly force on the furry animals. They didn't have any canteen going to bed.

Later on that night when everybody was asleep, Robert steps out of his tent to take a piss. He pisses and startles a skunk that was just as scared as him. Robert accidentally pisses on his boxers, and the skunk sprays him. He gets so offended by the skunk, he runs back to the tent and grabs his gun. He goes back to where the skunk was and start shooting.

The noise awakens Linda, Shawn, and the rest of the birds sleeping. The smell on Robert left an awful odor in the tent for the rest of the night. The next morning, the scent was still there. The family was hungry and had nothing to eat. Robert wants to go coon hunting. In the state park, you're not supposed to hunt animals. Robert felt since it ate his food, he's going to eat it.

Robert couldn't think properly, his head hurt, and he didn't want to talk to his wife. All he saw was a dead raccoon.

He has a little bit of a mental issue. When Robert spot a raccoon, he put 2 to the head and 1 to the chest and cook it. They go swimming until evening and the Peckerwoods go on a hike through the woods. They each carry a flashlight on the trail. While they're walking, Shawn finds some duck eggs and immediately smashes them against a tree stomp. Linda tells Shawn those eggs weren't bothering him and to quit being so barbaric.

They come to a clearing and decide to build a fire and tell ghost stories. Shawn is building a small fire and ends up pouring gasoline on the flames. The flame burst's and catches the gas can on fire. Shawn throws the container and it makes a line of fire through the woods. Robert and Linda run and stomp out the flames before it started to spread. Shawn burned his hand in the process. Robert tells the story first about the legend of the mini lights. Shawn has never heard of them before. He tells him about a voodoo witch who lived here in Historic Woods. She had little creatures who would do anything she asked. Robert says kids come out in these woods and never return. The witch put a curse in these woods. It's rich in urban history in this part of town.

Shawn starts telling his dad it's not real and it's just a legend along with Santa Claus. Robert starts chanting, "Mini lights, mini lights, come out tonight, mini lights, mini lights, come out tonight." Shawn is telling his dad he's freaking him out. Robert stops, and it gets eerily quiet and spooky. Robert keeps telling the story about an old woman named Minnie Lightning that had a house in the deepest parts of the woods.

"And that these woods are cursed." From a distance within the woods, the Peckerwood family sees little green balls of light. The air was dry and still. The hair on Shawn's arm was standing straight up. Shawn lets out a frightened cat scream. They all know it's time to go. They find out the woods are haunted. It was one of Florida's most haunted places.

They pack their things and haul ass down the trail by the old creek. It felt like they were never going to get out the woods. Shortly after they lost track of the trail and had to stop. Robert started hearing strange noises all around them. Linda was freaking out, they were lost. The batteries in the flashlights are flickering. Panic is setting in. Robert and Linda start yelling at each other about whose fault it was that they were lost. They get to a creek where they could hear civilization.

The creek is too dangerous to cross due to alligators. They couldn't see anything. They are yelling for help and another group of campers actually heard them. They saw a fire signal and call for a park ranger who calls for a search and rescue. The Peckerwoods were dehydrated and hungry. A helicopter rescue team air lifts them out of the woods to the nearest hospital. The helicopter pilot told them that in the dark, they would not have found their way out. When the Peckerwoods return home and pull in their driveway, they notice mangos missing from their tree and someone had broken into their house.

Track 5

Jit Wars

Abraham Park has been shot up and Tyrone and his friends were nearly killed. So, they need all the guns they can get. If you ask them, they don't sell guns. None of the boys have big homies. They are their own big homies. Tyrone and his friends chill on the bench at the park. Nick was talking about going to First Friday tomorrow.

Every First Friday of the month is when jits pile up at the movies. While they were talking, a car drives by real slow. They all clutch their straps, but it was nobody. They were looking for a house. Everyone is just paranoid as shit.

They chill for a little while longer, when Tyrone eventually go to Pooh Pooh's house. She lives next to the park. That's his lil boo, and she loves his ass. But they always fight. Pooh Pooh will fight Tyrone back like a nigga. She isn't scared. They have their little problems, but they love each other. Pooh Pooh's sister, Ariel is Fatty's baby mama.

The other 3 boys sit at the park talking a bit, when Nick takes one of the lil boys bikes without asking and rides home. They were on the court playing basketball. Niggas hate that shit. You can't let anybody borrow your bike either. Next time you see them, they won't have your bike. They hide it every time they come to the hood so you won't get it. Thug and Bre hang out for a while then bust off.

Tyrone stayed the night at his girlfriend's house. He didn't even go home. Floesha stopped caring about what he do. She gave up on him too early. Pooh Pooh's mama likes Tyrone. She didn't mind him staying over. It was like a second house for him. Tyrone can sleep in Pooh Pooh's room if he want. When they wake up and have sex, Tyrone smokes a joint and watch stand up comedy.

He catches the midnight rush on his phone. He walks back home early in the morning. Tyrone gets to the house and knocks on the door. Dae Dae went to the front who is it he stuttered. "Tyrone," then opens the door for his brother and lets him in. The whole house asleep. Tyrone goes into the kitchen to get something to drink. He has to move dishes that are stacked on each other to find a cup. Tyrone making noise moving them. They have a lot of pickle jars they use as cups. He washes it out and fills water from the faucet into it. He goes into the kitchen drawer. It is so raggedy, it creaks every time you open it to get something. Tyrone walks to the bathroom to take a shower.

After his shower, he gets out and puts on the same shorts and shirt. The only thing he changed was his stank ass drawers. He had his clothes on for days. Socks are crusty and moldy at the bottom from wearing them too much. He puts them back on when they are only $2 bucks at the corner store. Tyrone has a bad habit at running into the side of the wall in his house. He blames his house for being too small or maybe he's too clumsy. He is ready for school. He puts his paintball gun in his backpack. The last time he was at his bus stop, kids on another bus felt they had to throw paper balls at Tyrone for no reason. He doesn't even know any of them. So, Tyrone wants revenge. He is all loaded up and ready. He leaves his house without telling anyone and walks to the bus stop.

Tyrone go to the bus stop where all the kids stand. He has a mothafuckin plan. Tyrone think he's the man. As soon as he sees the bus, he shoots at the windows. Most likely, the windows will be down. Somebody was going to get splattered with orange paint. Sgt. Tyrone was ready for war. All the kids were standing around talking and waiting on the bus. It should be coming soon. Tyrone spots the bus he wants to get. It's from another school coming down the road. He gets his paintball gun into position. The bus from the other school always passes by right before his bus comes. He pulls his paintball gun from his side and starts shooting at the kids standing up on the bus. Tyrone lit up the kids who were standing. The windows were open, and he got their asses. All the children at the bus stop started laughing. They were standing in people yard waiting on the bus to come.

The bus eventually arrives and they get on. Tyrone and his friends go to the back of the bus. All that fighting Rosa Parks did for these kids, and they still go to the back of the bus all the time. That was the best part of the bus. Tyrone thought Rosa Parks fought for the wrong seats. When everyone is seated, Jesus takes off to Pineburg Middle School. On the way, some kid thought it would be funny to open the back emergency exit door. The door made a loud buzzing noise when it was open. Jesus didn't say anything. He just kept on driving. These kids run the bus. Eventually, the door shut. They were super loud, cussing with no respect on their way to school.

As the kids were getting off the bus in the bus circle, a boy name, Doo Doo wants to fight Javarias for rapping on the bus about who got the longest hair. The winner was going to get $20 bones. They pull their hair and Javarias lost. It went to the middle of his eyes and nose. Doo Doo pulled his, and it touched his lip. Doo Doo wants to fight when they get off because Javarias doesn't want to pay him. Doo Doo walks up to Javarias, and Javarias punches him 3 times in the eyeball. Doo Doo hair was in a ponytail and his rubber band went flying through the air.

Doo Doo grabs Javarias and slams him in the bus circle. All the kids form a circle around the two fighting. Administrators and O.C run over and breaks up the fight, telling everyone to get to class. The kids were saying that Javarias got beat up. Temetrius was a middle school bully. He had stayed back twice in the 8th grade. He's 16 trying to fight 13 and 14 year olds. He thinks he runs the campus. The teachers are going to kick his ass out of school if he don't pass to the next grade.

Temetrius talk like he can whip everybody's ass. One time, he loudly told a 12 year old he was going to make his lip fat, trying to cause a scene. Lemon Head got tired of Temetrius slapping his head and whips his ass. His ass whooping is long overdue. That was the last of Temetrius's rampage. Pineburg Middle was basically a predominately black school at the time. A lot of the black kids in the neighborhood went there. The school grade was an F. Tyrone goes to first period.

He hated coming to Mr. Cardwell's math class. It was his toughest subject. Tyrone would learn something and come back to school, high and forget. Mr. Cardwell felt weed was killing his brain cells.

"Tyrone, you're in my class."

"Dis my class, ain't it?" Tyrone responded.

"Oh yeah, I forgot. You're right. It's been a while. Glad you decided to grace us with your presence today, Tyrone. Everyone please take a seat. You missed a lot on your vacation. Did you visit county?"

"I went to yo mama's house wit yo lil head ass," Tyrone said. He sat down next to a girl named, Ebony. She hates Tyrone. He is always farting next to her so she could smell it. He gets on her nerves so much, she thought about bringing a knife to school to stab his ass. Tyrone has no respect. He always rides her black chucks. She wears them with different color shoe strings to match her clothes everyday.

Mr. Cardwell teaches the class math problems on the projector. Tyrone mocks how the teacher talks. Mr. Cardwell had a stroke, so he talks sideways with his lips. Tyrone always needs help with his work so he cheats. He shows off his first tattoo to one of his classmates on his forearm. The tattoo said Pine Boy. A friend got tatted with the same tattoo needle as him. Jazmina told Tyrone his tattoo looks crooked as hell and it's fucked up. It looks like a buddy did it.

Mr. Cardwell class was about over and he's distracted by helping other students on their work. Tyrone goes to the back of the classroom where Mr. Cardwell keeps his personal items.

Tyrone and Doo Doo grabs his laptop and camera. They put the stolen equipment in their backpacks. They caught Mr. Cardwell slipping. The bell rings and Tyrone walks to 2nd period. Mr. Cardwell didn't notice right away that his shit was gone. As soon as he found out, they call the school resource officer to Tyrone's classroom. They want to talk to Tyrone. Doo Doo had already told on his self and Tyrone because he got caught. Mr. Cardwell just wanted his laptop and camera back. He wasn't going to press charges.

Tyrone were in the gym's classroom on the laptop. To avoid going to JDC, he just gave the computer back to O.C. Mr. Frankel has to lecture Tyrone about his dress code again and how it's a major part of his grade. He never dresses out, and he doesn't give a shit about his grade.

Nick comes over to tell Tyrone about the food fight that's going to happen in lunch. A kid named, Corey was going to start it. The word was traveling fast amongst the students before it could even happen. An ambulance pulls up in front of the school.

All the kids run to the window to watch the boy who cut off the tip of his finger, trying to copycat another student from the year before. The kid cut the tip of his finger off with a paper cutter, sued the school and won. Tyrone was called to the 7th grade administrator's office, which was in a portable.

He gets there and Mrs. Fabrizio talks to Tyrone about his behavior and attendance. When she was finished talking to him, the devil whispers in Tyrone's ear to pull the fire extinguisher. He does it right in front of Mrs. Fabrizio. The room was clouded in foam.

So, the whole portable has to evacuate. After everyone cleared out, they had to put a giant fan in the office to help blow out the fumes. Tyrone got a white note and can only come back to school if his mama came in for a conference. Tyrone doesn't care. He leaves the portable and goes to lunch.

2nd period was over with. Nick met Tyrone inside the cafeteria. One of the lunch ladies doesn't pay attention to the kids. So, Tyrone is going to steal a cookie or ice cream. He gets in line and waits for a good time to swipe a cookie before he gets up to the lunch lady. He gives her his student number and goes to sit at the long table. Tyrone and his group of friends were all eating and talking. About 15 minutes into lunch, everybody is watching Corey. All of a sudden, Corey gets up and tosses his food at another student. It was on from there.

Everyone got up screaming, yelling, and throwing food everywhere. Pineburg Middle School was actually having a food fight. Several administrators came in the lunchroom and stopped it. The cafeteria was trashed. Corey was taken to the office in handcuffs by the school resource officer. The rest of the kids had to leave the lunch room.

Finally it's the end of the day and the last period bell rang. Tyrone gets on the bus ready to go home. On the way, he keeps switching seats, while listening to music on his phone. He raps out Loud. One kid calls him a sick ass nigga for wiping his boogers on the back of a seat. The white note Ms. Fabrizio wrote Tyrone was balled up and thrown out the window.

It was the First Friday of the month. Tyrone and his friends are going to the movies tonight. But before they go, they want to go hit a clothing store. The windows have no bars. It was on the north side on the main road. All someone has to do is throw something to break the window. The owner thinks his business is safe since it's on main street and in sheriff city.

Tyrone skips his house and doesn't check in. He goes straight to his friends' house where they plan to steal a van. Thug and Bre have a flathead screw driver to splack the cars. They are really quick at getting cars. Nick is the better driver than Tyrone. Last time, Tyrone drove them into a golf course. So, Nick will drive this time.

He knows how to dick troll. So, Tyrone and Nick are going to another neighborhood to get a car to steal. While Thug and Bre are going by the hospital to look, they wait until it gets dark before they head out on foot. They need two cars for the movies. Tyrone and Nick was having a hard time getting a car. One has a kill switch and another had a auto theft lock on the steering wheel. Thug and Bre found a car in the hospital parking lot.

They drive back to meet up with Tyrone and Nick. When they pull up in a stolo, they were blasting the speakers. The car tires was smelling like burnt rubber from driving so fast. Tyrone and Nick jump in and they went to the north to go hit the clothes store. Thug pulls up in front of the store and they all get out. Bre picks up a rock he saw and smashes the window to the store.

It shatters. The alarm goes off. Everyone runs in and starts grabbing clothes. They were in and out and everybody had plenty of new clothes. They all jump back in the car and drive towards the highway. They can see the sheriff's lights reflect through the back window. Thug jet back to the hood. The lick was successful. They were fast made it out safe and long gone before the sheriff came. When they get back, they show off what they got and get fresh for the movies.

Tyrone and Nick ride with Thug and Bre in the stolen car to the movies. Some of their friends from the hood couldn't fit so the rest ride bikes to the movies. They hid their bikes in bushes, while Thug and Bre parked their car in a apartment parking lot. Everyone is calling each other meeting up. When Tyrone and his friends get there, the movies are on smash. It's always deep on First Fridays.

Tyrone and the others walk the sidewalks. Jits are everywhere. No one actually goes inside the movies. They just go to post up. A lot of different hoods were out there so it was only a matter of time for something to happen. The police were everywhere. Cross was there too. They were super deep. Trap Monkey, Lil' D, and Nut know who Tyrone is. They are ready. People don't mind going to jail at the movies. The police are trying to get teens to move off the sidewalk. Someone refused and was arrested and put into a patty wagon.

Lil' D spot Abraham Park and seen them only 8 deep. Cross Boys start talking shit to Abraham Park Boys. AP was talking shit right back. Cross get up on Abraham Park and they all started fighting. Lil niggas and big niggas were jumping Tyrone. Some of Tyrone's friends help him fight and some didn't.

P.A. Bricks fought against Cross trying to help Abraham Park. There were too many police for the fight to last long. They came in pepper spraying. The police made everyone clear out from in front of the court yard. These jits don't know how to hang and chill, always fighting. Tyrone, Nick, Thug, and Bre all go to their car and head back to the hood. They were all heated. They all felt like Cross just tried them. Tyrone wants get back. They wanted to pull out their guns but didn't do it because of the police.

Tyrone and his homeboys went to the hood's park. They want to go shoot that shit up. Too many people trying them like they won't do anything. Tyrone, Nick, and Thug all got their own flames ready to Chicken Wing Flame. Cross feels good about jumping on Tyrone at the movies. They got off on them and they know it. Cross wasn't thinking anything about the incident, that was left at the movies. Cross went back across town to their neighborhood. Tyrone was going to see about that. They load up 4 deep dressed in all black. Lil Nick speed cross town and drive through Cross. Tyrone, Thug, and Bre open their car doors and stick their guns out the window. Pop, pop, pop, pop, pop, pop, pop. They open fire on Cross standing in a group at a house. Nobody couldn't see the shooters because it happened so fast.

Those niggas started running from a hail of bullets. The neighbors came out the door and called the ambulance. This was the first to a Jit War. This new generation isn't fighting any more. Some niggas ran to the next house over and got away while another ducked and one got shot in the back close range. Nick flush down the road. All you can hear is the rubber on the tires, speeding off. Them lil niggas were not playing. They straight wetting shit. AP wants respect and niggas were going to start respecting them. They tell you one time they are going to fight, but after that, Abraham Park taking it to gunplay.

They aren't with all that fighting. Word spread that one of Abraham Park Boys put one of the Cross Boys in a wheel chair and paralyzed him. Cross Boys don't retaliate right away. Tyrone gets back to the hood. They go to an alley and post up. There's several sections in the hood they post at. The park, alley, store, and car wash. Tyrone calls one of his friends from P.A. Bricks and tell them over the phone what went down, who was with who, and what kind of guns they had, talking crazy on a police phone.

P.A Bricks gets cool with Abraham Park and started calling themselves Abraham Bricks. The 2 hoods started going places with each other. P.A Bricks was beefing with The Dale, Pine Dale neighborhood. They were shooting at each other. Ever since someone got shot by APN and every time there's a shooting, Abraham Park would get the blame for it. People would throw their name in everything. At one point, Abraham Park wasn't invited to block parties because everybody thought they would shoot up the party it got so bad.

Pineburg Police have been getting some names from hoes on the street. Bitches talk. Tyrone and Charles are a couple of the names that have been ringing bells lately. The police want to talk to the both of them. Their names have been in everything going down. The police want to speak to Thug about numerous robberies, burglaries, and grand theft autos. Tyrone wanted for questioning about a couple of shootings and burglarizes.

People in the community feared Tyrone. The ladies love a hot boy. Thug is a teenager with older women and kids. Niggas was so scared of Abraham Park that they would definitely snitch in a MOTHAFUCKIN heartbeat. A lot of hoes hated Abraham Park.

On the 6 o'clock news, Tyrone and Thug's mug shots were put up claiming these two men are considered armed and dangerous and are wanted in connection with a shooting that happened at a park. Tyrone's cousin took him to go fight some niggas and Tyrone wound up shooting in front of everybody, even though it was his cousin's fight.

Everybody knows who Tyrone is and told on him. Tyrone and his friend didn't turn themselves in. They were going to make the police do their job. They hid at Thug's grandma's house. They know it's only a matter of time. They drop their guns off at a friend's house who stays in the neighborhood.

Tyrone washed the gun powder residue off his arms. He doesn't go home because he knows the police would come looking for him there. The police raid all the blocks around the hood, looking for Tyrone and Charles. They are passing out wanted flyers door to door, bleeding the neighborhood. They get a call a couple hours after being out. It was a tip saying Tyrone and Charles might be hiding at Charles grandma's house. The lead was right.

They found the boys. Charles' grandma had let the police in to arrest both juveniles. PWN News Station was there. Tyrone told the news to suck his dick, "I Din Do Nuffin." Tyrone and Charles made the 10 o'clock news. The two were arrested and taken into custody.

Vice squad is getting ready to conduct an illegal drug raid on Pookie's drug house. The male later identified as Nathaniel

"Fatty" Jones, a convicted felon, is suspected of dealing narcotics out his home. "We don't want it in our neighborhoods and in our city. It's a crack house," said Trigg. Pineburg narcotic agents put their gear on and head out to the subject's prior location. The narcs riding deep. They leave the police station and drive through the neighborhoods. People on social media posting be safe them boys out. Giving others a heads up on the police.

They drive to Abraham Park neighborhood. Rambo and Superman saw some kids standing at the store, when it says no loitering and rush. The teens tried to power walk into the store and ditch their drugs. Some couldn't run so the narcs grab them and search them.

Superman went after the boy going into the store and grabs him. He already had his ID in his hand, but Superman didn't give a fuck about that and takes him outside, searches him and finds marijuana. Rambo has his knee in someone's back on the ground. The narcs were fucking with people in the neighborhood, telling them they couldn't stand at the store.

Quant was lucky. He's older and from the hood who sold weed out of his car at the store all the time. He left just in time. Narcs rushed the store and race to Pookie's house. Police surround the front. Trigg park his cruiser in the back with multiple narcotic agents. They rush the yard. Fatty was in the house, flushing drugs down the toilet immediately. He had nowhere to run.

There was drug paraphernalia all over the house. It's a trap just like the name. Bitches tried to run in the house. Police raid the house arresting the mechanic and everybody standing in the yard. Fatty was arrested and taken outside to be searched. Vice squad didn't have forensics. They collect the drugs themselves and a large sum of money an keeps it.

The people who were in the recording studio were searched. One of the jits kept talking shit to the police, and Trigg searches the boy and plant drugs on him. The police officers who searched them knew they didn't have any drugs when they searched but did nothing or said nothing when Trigg searched.

Vice agents search the rest of the house for drugs. Fatty was placed in a police cruiser and Trigg did the paperwork on him. Everybody in the neighborhood was outside watching the drug bust go down. Police had masks on and in all black so you couldn't recognize any of their faces. A woman came up asking questions about what happened, and a neighbor told her Pookie's house got hit.

Tyrone was so bad his name made the radio station because he broke in too many people houses in Pine County. Society calls him an endangerment to others.

Made in the USA
Columbia, SC
22 February 2020

88105828R10055